Enid Blyton's

HEDGEROW TALES

Illustrated by
Frances Stevens

HUTCHINSON

LONDON · MELBOURNE · AUCKLAND · JOHANNESBURG

Produced by Templar Publishing Ltd,
Old King's Head Court, Dorking, Surrey, RH4 1AR,
for Hutchinson Children's Books

Text copyright © Darrell Waters Limited 1935
Illustrations copyright © Templar Publishing 1986

These stories have been taken from *Hedgerow Tales*, first published
in 1935 by Methuen Children's Books
This edition first published 1986 by Hutchinson Children's Books
An imprint of Century Hutchinson Ltd
Brookmount House, 62–65 Chandos Place, Govent Garden,
London WC2N 4NW

Century Hutchinson Group (Australia) Pty Ltd,
16–22 Church Street, Hawthorn, Melbourne, Victoria 3122

Century Hutchinson Group (NZ) Ltd,
32–34 View Road, PO Box 40–086, Glenfield, Auckland 10

Century Hutchinson Group (SA) Pty Ltd,
PO Box 337, Bergvlei 2012, South Africa

Set in Souvenir Light by Kalligraphics Ltd

Colour separations by Positive Colour Ltd, Maldon, Essex
Printed and bound in Great Britain by Purnell
Book Production Ltd, Paulton, Bristol
Member of BPCC plc

British Library Cataloguing in Publication Data

Blyton, Enid
    Enid Blyton's hedgerow tales.
    I. Title   II. Stevens, Frances
    823'.921 (J)   PZ7
    ISBN 0–09–167250–3

CONTENTS

RABBITY WAYS

The night had been very dark, for there was no moon. Now there was a grey light creeping into the eastern sky. Daybreak was near. Soon the owls would go home and the bats would fly back to the old barn to sleep. The oak tree that grew out of the hedgerow rustled its leaves in the chilly wind. It was a wise old tree, friendly to all creatures, and loved by a great many.

The hedgerow was old, too. In it grew hawthorn, whose leaves were out early in the spring-time, green fingers held up to the sun. Bramble sprays flung long arms here and there, as prickly as the wild rose that forced its way up to the sun. Ivy covered one part of the hedge, and here, in blossom-time, feasted the last late flies and many beautiful red admirals.

Below was a sunny bank, for the hedgerow faced south. In summer-time the birds found wild strawberries on this bank, and the primroses sometimes flowered there in the early days of January. In the ditch below there was moss growing, soft as velvet, and a few graceful ferns. It was always damp there and cool.

Near the old oak tree was a small pond, ringed round with rushes and meadow-sweet. Many creatures came to drink there – from the sly red fox down to the striped yellow wasp! All the creatures in the fields around knew the pond well, and often the swallows would come and skim above it, looking for flies.

The hedgerow was in a deserted corner of the field. Nobody came there, not even the children hunting for blackberries. The farmer had forgotten to cut the hedge for years, and it had grown tall and tangled. Sometimes the wind would bring the sound of the farmer's voice, shouting to his horses in a distant field, but usually the hedgerow knew nothing but the sound of the wind, of bird calls and pattering paws.

Many, many things had happened in and around the hedgerow. The oak tree had rustled its leaves over thousands of insects, birds and animals. Its twigs knew the difference between a squirrel's scampering paws and a bird's light hold. Its acorns had been stolen by all kinds of mice, and by the screeching jays and the hungry nuthatch.

Now it stood whispering in the cool wind of daybreak. Summer was passing over, and soon the oak leaves would lose their dark green hue and would turn brown.

The grey light in the sky became brighter. Beneath the oak tree, where the bank showed a sandy streak, a hole could just be seen. It was a rabbit's burrow. The burrow went down among the roots of the tree, exactly the size of a rabbit's body except now and again when it widened out to make passing-places for two meeting rabbits. The tunnel branched off into two or three different burrows, but the rabbits had learnt every foot of them, and always knew which tunnel to take when they wanted to go to the gorse bush, to the bank or to the other side of the pond.

Out of the hole in the bank a rabbit's head appeared. Her big eyes looked through the dim grey light, her nose twitched as she sniffed the air, and her big ears listened to every sound. She wanted to go out and feed on the grass, and she had with her a young family of five rabbits, who were just getting old enough to look after themselves.

'It is safe,' she said to her young ones. We can go out. There is no stoat about, and the owls have all gone home.'

They trooped out of the hole. Other rabbits were in the field too, big ones and little ones, for there were many burrows there.

'Keep near the burrow,' said the mother rabbit. 'Then you will not have far to run if danger comes. I am going along the hedgerow. There is a young furze bush there and I shall feed on the juicy shoots. Keep an eye on the other rabbits, and if you see them turn so that their white bobtail shows plainly, dart into your burrow. Bobbing tails mean danger somewhere! And keep your ears pricked, too – for if one of the old rabbits scents danger he will drum on the ground with his hind foot to warn us all. Then you must run as fast as you can.'

The little rabbits began to nibble the grass. They felt quite sure they could look after themselves. Their mother ran silently along the hedgerow. Suddenly she stopped and stood so still that it seemed as if she had frozen stiff. She had seen another animal coming through the hedge. It was a brown hare. As soon as the rabbit saw that it was a harmless creature, she ran on towards it. 'You scared me, cousin hare,' she said. 'Is your burrow round here?'

'Burrow!' said the hare, looking in surprise at the rabbit, her soft eyes gleaming in the grey light. 'I have no burrow. I live above the ground.'

'But how dangerous!' said the rabbit in alarm. 'Stoats and weasels could easily find you! Do you make a nest like the birds?'

'Come with me,' said the hare. 'I will show you where I live. My home is called a form, because it is simply a dent in the ground the size and form of my body. I make it the shape of my body by lying in it, you see. I like to live alone. I should not like to live with others, as you do.'

'But it is safer,' said the rabbit, going with the hare over the field. 'I have left my young ones with the other rabbits, and they will warn them if danger is near. There is safety in numbers.'

'My ears and my nose make me safe,' said the hare. 'I can smell far-away things and hear the slightest noise. Look at my ears. They are longer than yours, cousin. See the black tips, too. You have no black tips. Look at my hind legs. Yours are strong, but mine are much stronger. I can run like the wind!'

Suddenly the hare gave a great leap, and jumped many feet over the field. The rabbit was startled, but the hare called to her.

'Here is my form. I always jump like that before I go to it, so that I break my trail. Then if weasel or stoat come round they cannot follow my scent, for it breaks where I jump! Come here, cousin. I have some young ones to show you. They are only a few days old.'

The rabbit went to the hare's form. Near it were other small holes, and in each lay a young hare, a leveret, its eyes wide open, its body warmly covered with fur.

'They have made forms of their own,' said the hare, proudly. 'Even when they are young they like to live alone.'

'My young ones were not like this,' said the rabbit in surprise, looking at the leverets. 'My children were born blind and deaf and had no fur on them at all. I made a special burrow for them, and blocked up the entrance to it every time I went out. I should not think of leaving them out in the open like this. It is a good thing

your children are born able to see and hear, or they would certainly be eaten by an enemy!'

'They are safe enough,' said the hare. 'Now take me to your home, cousin rabbit. I would like to see your youngsters, too.'

The two animals went back to the hedgerow. The hare gave another great leap when she left her form. It was a favourite trick of hers not only when leaving her home, but when she was hunted by dogs. Sometimes she would double on her tracks, too, to throw off her hunters. It nearly always deceived them.

The hare was astonished to see the burrow in which the rabbits lived. 'But how do you manage about your ears?' she asked. 'Do you bend them back when you run underground? 'That must be very uncomfortable. It is a strange idea to tunnel in the earth. I am sure that our family were not meant to do so, or we would not have been given such long ears. It must be difficult, too, to dig out all the earth.'

'No, it is easy,' said the rabbit, 'I dig with my front paws and shovel out the earth with my hind paws. See, cousin, there are my children feeding over there.'

The hare was looking at the young rabbits in the light of the dawn when a curious noise came to her long ears. It was a drumming sound, and it seemed to the hare as if the ground were quivering under her feet. The mother rabbit called to her young ones at once.

'Come here! There is danger about! That is the old rabbit drumming with his hind feet to warn us. Come, cousin, you must hide in our burrow, too.'

The young rabbits lifted their heads when they heard the drumming. Then they saw all the other rabbits running in every direction to their holes, their white bobtails showing clearly. In seconds the young ones were off, too, scampering to their hole. Not a rabbit was to be seen when the old red fox came slinking by. The hare had gone, too – but not down the burrow.

'My legs are safer than a burrow!' she thought to herself. 'I shall run, not hide! No fox can catch *me*!'

'Poor hare!' thought the rabbit. 'She ought to dig a burrow, then she would be safe. The fox will surely get her.'

But the fox went hungry that morning!

THE END

PRICKLY
FRIENDS

There were many holes in the bank under the hedgerow. Some were big, some were small, but nearly all of them had some creature living there. A hole made a safe and warm hiding-place, a home to come back to after wanderings in the fields. The leaves of the oak tree knew all the holes, for they drifted there when they fell, or were taken into them by the little creatures who wanted to line the holes for winter nests.

There was one very nice hole, tucked under a jutting-out piece of bank so that it could hardly be seen. It did not look very big from the outside, because a curtain of moss hung over the entrance. But inside it was very roomy. It had been dug out the summer before by a colony of wasps. The queen wasp had started the hole and, when her first eggs had hatched into grubs and then into wasps, her children had helped her to make the hole bigger and bigger to hold the growing nest.

But one night the big badger had come prowling by and had smelt out the wasps. He liked the taste of the fat wasp grubs, so he put his big clawed foot into the hole and scraped until he had the nest out.

It was a grey, papery
thing, full of eggs, grubs and live wasps.
They were frightened of this attack in the dark, and
although they tried hard to sting the badger they
could not pierce his thick hide.

He ate all the eggs and grubs and destroyed so many of the
wasps that the nest was not rebuilt again and the hole was
deserted. A mouse went in and finished up what was left of the
nest, and when the autumn came the wind blew in a great heap
of oak leaves. The little mouse used the hole as a larder, and
stored there a hazelnut and two acorns.

He was there one day in summer when he heard a snuffling
in the damp ditch below. Then a pig-like snout was suddenly
pushed into the hole and the mouse sat frozen with fright. It was a
hedgehog! It had been raining, and the rain had brought out the
worms and slugs, so the hedgehog had woken early from her
daytime sleep and had gone hunting.

Now a hedgehog thinks nothing of making a meal of a small
brown mouse, and the tiny creature thought his last moment had
come. But the hedgehog was very full of worms and slugs, and
she had no room for a mouse just then. So when she withdrew
her snout from the hole, the mouse rushed out thankfully and ran
to another hole in the field, making up his mind never, never to
go back to his larder-hole again.

The hedgehog smelt the mouse-smell in the hole and was

sorry she could not manage another meal. She went back to the ditch and snuffled about for a little while longer. She usually liked to hunt in the twilight of evening, or dawn, but she was full with her meal of worms and slugs and did not want to hunt anymore.

She felt instead she would like to examine the hole she had seen, for soon she would want a home for a family. She decided to go and have a look round the hole, and if it was a suitable place, she would take it for her own. She could get it ready that night. It was a nice hedgerow to live in, high and unclipped, with a big tree overshadowing it. The moist ditch underneath was a fine place for hunting, and the pond nearby would give her water to drink.

She went back to the hole. It was sunset and the sky was full of red banked-up clouds. The mouse was gone, of course. The hedgehog pushed her way in. It was a tight fit at the entrance, but inside the hole was quite roomy. There were dead oak leaves there, dry and brittle, from last autumn, and two acorn shells and a gnawed hazelnut. The hedgehog turned round and round in the hole, and then lay down with her snout pointing towards the entrance, so that she could see if anyone came by. The moss hung down a little to hide it, but she could see the evening light outside, filtering into the hole. It was a good hole.

'It shall be mine,' thought the hedgehog. 'Here I will bring up my children, for there will be plenty of food in the ditch for them. They will be safe here.'

When the little mouse ventured near to the hole one day in August he heard a strange noise coming from it – a hoarse sound that came and went as he listened. Whatever could it be?

He crept nearer, and was at last bold enough to push aside the mossy curtain and look in. One peep was enough! He fled down the bank and threw himself into the tall stinging nettles. The hedgehog was there – fast alseep and snoring, it is true, but with her were wide-awake children, their beady eyes sharply watching the entrance of their home!

'The hole I used for my winter-larder is taken by a hedgehog and her family,' the little mouse told the rabbit that lived down the burrow under the oak tree. 'Go and see.'

The rabbit was interested to hear of the newcomers, and she watched to see who came from the hole in the bank. She had not long to wait, for one fine September night, just when it was dusk and the moon was rising, the hedgehog put her snout out of the hole and, after she had snuffed the air, came out quickly. Behind her came seven curious little creatures, with short grey spines – her children.

The hedgehog saw the watching rabbit at once, but did not fear her. She set about hunting for food, and very soon crunched up a few beetles, one worm, a big snail, and a small green frog. The little hedgehogs ran about like clockwork, their short legs twinkling underneath them. They rooted out beetles, and were pleased to find slugs eating a toadstool.

'Keep near me,' called their mother, warningly. 'The badger may be about, or the fox, and remember you cannot roll up into a ball yet as I can. You will not be able to until you are a year old, so be careful until then.'

'How do you roll up?' asked the rabbit, looking at the hedgehog's prickly body. 'Show me.'

At once the hedgehog curled herself up so tightly that she looked exactly like a round ball of prickles. Her head was hidden, and she lay as still as stone. Soon she unrolled herself and looked proudly at the rabbit.

'I am well armoured!' she said. 'I am afraid of few enemies — the badger, perhaps, and the fox.'

'But surely the fox can't eat you,' said the rabbit, trembling a little at the mention of her cunning enemy. 'Your prickles would make his mouth bleed.'

'He can only get me if I
unroll myself,' said the hedgehog,
'and he makes me uncurl by a very horrible trick. He is an evil-
smelling creature when he likes, and as I cannot bear him at his
smelliest, I uncurl to get away. Then he can catch me easily. But
my short, sharp prickles make all other creatures drop me in a
hurry if they try to eat me!'

'I wish I had your spines!' said the rabbit, longingly. 'But I
only have my strong, swift legs to help me when enemies are
near.'

Suddenly there came the sound of a pitiful wail through the
dusk. The hedgehog scuttled towards it at once, for she knew the
cry of her young ones. The rabbit bolted headlong into her hole,
and all the rabbits nearby did the same.

'Badger! Badger!' murmured all the creatures of the
hedgerow, lying low with their ears well pricked and their eyes
bright. 'Badger! He has come down from the hills.'

The hedgehog met her young ones hurrying towards her —
but one was gone.

'A great creature suddenly came upon us,' said the young
hedgehogs, shaking with fear. 'He had heavy clawed feet, and his
muzzle was pointed. He ate one of us. Let us go to our hole
before he comes after us.'

The mother hedgehog pushed her children before her and they ran to the hedgerow as fast as they could on their short feet. All their prickles bristled as they ran, though the spines of the young ones were soft compared with their mother's. They clambered up the bank and one by one squeezed into the hole, the mother following last of all. The small hedgehogs cuddled close to her, although she was not a comfortable mother to love. There they all lay, their hearts beating fast, remembering the little hedgehog who cried so pitifully as the badger caught him.

One little hedgehog began to squeak with fright as he remembered.

'Hush,' warned the mother. 'The badger may come this way. Listen! You can hear the thud of his heavy tread.'

They all listened, snug in their hole, the night sky outside lit up by the silver moon. The badger was looking for another meal, for he was hungry. He decided to hunt for mice and came along the ditch, his heavy feet scuffling the leaves as he walked. The hedgehogs lay breathless in their hole. If the badger smelt them, it would not be long before all the young ones, at least, were eaten.

There were no mice to be found. The badger raised his snout

in the air and sniffed. He thought he smelt a faint scent of
hedgehog. Then a sound startled him and he lumbered off over
the field, away from the hedgerow. He was gone.

'Come out,' said the rabbit, appearing at the hedgehog's
hole. 'The moon is in the sky, and the badger has gone. There is
good hunting for you tonight.'

But the hedgehogs did not stir abroad that night. The next
night they left their hole to find another, for they were afraid that
the badger might come back.

'Goodbye,' said the hedgehog to the rabbit. 'I shall see you
again, for when winter comes and I want to sleep, I shall come
back to that good hole, I think. It is so warm and comfortable, and
if I line it with leaves and moss it will make a fine sleeping-place.
Goodbye till then!'

Then away she went with her six prickly children, little grey
shadows in the moonlight.

THE END

THE ADVENTURERS

Octotober days had been sunny and warm, and there were many blackberries ripe in the hedgerow. Some of the bramble-leaves were turning scarlet and gold, and glowed brightly when the sun shone through them. The ivy was blooming on the hedge just below the oak tree, and to it came hundreds of bluebottle flies, butterflies, wasps, bees and little creeping insects. It was the last feast of the year before the long winter set in.

The swallows and the martins had revelled in the warm October sunshine, but they did not like the chilly nights. The oak tree felt the wind of their wings all day long as they flew round, for many of the insects that fed on the ivy flowers below flew up into the air when they were satisfied, and were chased and caught by the keen-eyed swallows. The martins, too, knew where the ivy blossom was, with its insects, and darted up and down over the hedge, catching unwary bluebottles as they buzzed noisily over the ivy.

The rabbits, peeping
out of their holes, knew the birds well. They had
arrived one April morning, when the south wind was
blowing strongly, a great crowd of them together, crying,
'Feetafeetit, feetafeetit' to one another. They were weary little
birds then, but very happy. They had flown a long way to come
to the fields they knew, for they all wished to nest in the spot they
had loved so well the year before.

'There is the oak tree!' they cried to one another as they
circled round it. 'And see, here is the hedgerow where the ivy
blooms later on! We are home again!'

Then off they flew to find the old barn where each year the
swallows built their nests, and the old farmhouse against which
the house-martins liked to put their homes of mud. It was lovely
to be home again after being away all the long winter. Now sunny
days, clouds of insects to eat, the joys of nesting and bringing up
young ones lay before them, and the little birds were happy.

The creatures of the hedgerow did not very often speak to
the flying swallows and martins, because, unlike other birds, they
seldom perched on trees or bushes. All day long they flew in the
air, and the rabbits grew used to their musical voices, twittering
from dawn to dusk.

24

When they were making their nests, two lizards who lived on the bank near the pond watched the pretty little birds in surprise – for both swallows and martins came down to the pond-side and scraped up mud in their beaks! The lizards thought at first that they were eating the mud, and wondered if there were insects in it.

'Why do you eat mud?' asked one lizard. 'It has no taste.'

The swallow could not answer because her beak was full of mud – but another swallow, who had just flown down to the pond-side, answered the lizard.

'We are not eating mud!' she said, with a twittering, laughing sound. 'We are taking it to build our nests.'

'But nests are not built of mud,' said the lizard, who had seen a robin building her nest in the hedgerow bank the year before, and thought he knew all about nests. 'They are built of roots, leaves and moss.'

'Not ours!' said the swallow. 'We make a saucer of mud on one of the beams of the old barn, and there we put our eggs, pretty white things with brown spots.'

'But doesn't the mud make your eggs dirty and wet?' asked the lizard.

'Of course not, cried the swallow, thinking that the lizard must be very stupid. 'It dries hard and makes a fine nest. See, I will put a beakful of mud by your hole on the bank. You will see that it gets quite hard when it dries.'

The swallow dropped some mud in a tiny pile beside the lizard's hole and then went back to the pond-side again, scooping up some more mud in her beak. Then off she flew to the barn away across the field to dab the mud against the growing saucer-nest she was building.

The martins came to the pond as often as the swallows, and the lizards grew to know them well whilst they were nest-building. But as soon as the nests were finished the twittering birds came no more to the pond-side, but flew high in the blue summer sky all the day. Once or twice they saw the little lizards and called gaily to them, but it was not until October came, with its chilly mornings and evenings, that the lizards saw the swallows to talk to once again.

Then they noticed that the telegraph wires that ran over the hedgerow, held up by a tall black pole, were quite weighted down with swallows and martins each evening. They seemed to be collecting together from all the fields around. The lizards looked at them in wonder. They could see the swallows with their steel-blue backs, long forked tails and chestnut-coloured throats, and they knew that the other birds, with shorter tails and a white patch at the lower end of

their backs, were the little house-martins.

Why were they all crowding together like this?

'Feetafeetit, feetafeetit!' cried the swallows. 'It is time to go!'

'Where to?' asked the lizards, calling out to a swallow that skimmed low over the pond, tryng to catch a fly.

'To a warmer land!' said the swallow. 'Come with us!'

'How far is it?' asked the lizard.

'Hundreds, thousands of miles!' cried the swallow. 'We fly with the north wind. We must go!'

'But why must you go?' asked the lizard. 'Don't go, swallow! We like to hear your twittering.'

'We are going to a land where there are plenty of insects,' said the swallow. 'If we stay here for the cold days, we would die of hunger.'

'No, you wouldn't,' said the lizard. 'The robin stays, and the thrush and blackbird, and *they* feed on insects. As a matter of fact, *I* feed on insects, too.'

'Ah, but *you* go to sleep in the winter!' said the swallow. 'I know you do , because one spring we came back early and the lizards were still asleep in their holes, the lazy creatures! But we *must* go, lizard – I don't really know why we have to go, and I don't know the way – but when this time of year comes and the north wind begins to blow, something stirs inside me, and I feel I must fly to the south for miles upon miles!'

'It is a great aventure,' said the lizard.

'The greatest adventure in the world!' answered the swallow. 'We fly together in a big flock over the sea and over the land, over mountains and rivers, fields and forests. And all the time we cry to one another, for we are afraid of getting lost, especially at night or in a fog.'

'What if a storm comes?' asked the lizard, trembling as he remembered a great storm that had happened in the summer.

'Ah, then we may perish!' said the swallow. 'But most of us get to the lands in the south, where the sun shines all day. We

love it, but it isn't our home. We don't nest there. It is just a holiday for us, that's all! We shall all be longing for the spring to come again, for then one day we shall feel homesick for the fields and hills round here, and when the south wind blows to help us, we shall go with it — back to the old barns we love so well! I shall

come back to my barn, and I will call to you as I dart over the hedgerow. Then you will know I have come back. You are sure you won't come with us?'

'How can I?' said the lizard, impatiently. 'I have no wings. Besides, I would be afraid. I am not used to adventuring as you are.'

'Then goodbye!' called the swallow, and flew up to join his brothers and sisters on the telegraph wires. The lizard heard him excitedly twittering as he told all that had been said. The other birds twittered back, and the evening air was full of their sweet, high voices.

'Thank goodness they're going!' said a robin, suddenly, looking out of the hedgerow. 'They eat too many insects. Food will soon get scarce. I would drive away those swallows if they stayed round here!'

'Don't get in a temper!' cried the swallows, hearing his high, creamy trill. 'We are going tonight, tonight, tonight!'

'The north wind is blowing!' twittered the martins. 'The sky is clear. It is time to go. We need not fly all the way at once. We can rest whenever we find good feeding-grounds, for the wind is behind us. Let us go tonight, tonight, tonight!'

The rabbits came out to watch, and the hare stood upright in the nearby field. The hedgehog and her young ones felt the excitement too. The two lizards peeped trembling from their hole. The feathered adventurers were going on their long journey! All the animals longed to share in it.

Suddenly, in their hundreds, the swallows flew into the evening air, circled round once or twice, and then, in a great cloud, flew towards the south. 'Feetafeetit, feetafeetit!' they called. 'Goodbye, goodbye! We will come back in the spring.'

They were gone. Soon not even the soft noise of their thousand wings could be heard. All the hedgerow creatures sighed and went back to their holes. They would miss the swallows and their bright voices – but the spring would bring them back again. Ah, but the spring was far away!

'What adventurers!' thought the rabbit, scuttling down her hole. 'What daring little adventurers!'

THE END

ONE
WARM WINTER'S
DAY

T he weather had been cold and frosty. The ground had
been as hard as iron, and when the bitter wintry wind blew,
the dead leaves in the ditch had made a dry, crackling
sound as they flew here and there. It had been hard weather for
all the creatures still awake – the rabbits and hares, the weasels
and stoats, the birds in the trees, the mice and the voles. They
were hungry and cold. Only the sleepers were happy.

The dormouse slept comfortably in his cosy hole. The lizard
and the newt knew nothing of the winter as they slept under the
shelter of a big stone. The hedgehog snored gently in the bank,
and the bat still hung upside down in a nearby cave, fast asleep.

A small, mouse-like creature poked his nose out of a hole in
the bank one winter's day. It was a little field-vole with a short tail.
He was not a mouse, for his body was rounded instead of long,
and his ears were very short. His muzzle was not pointed like a
mouse's, but was blunt. He sniffed the air before he came out
from his hole. He knew that weasels and stoats were about, fierce
with hunger, and he wanted to
make sure he was safe.

The sun shone down on to the hedgerow bank. It felt warm to the little vole. There was no frost that morning. The New Year had come in softly and the weather had changed. For a little while it would be warmer. The field-vole was glad. He had been hiding in his burrow underground for a few days. The last time he had ventured out he had nearly been caught by a hungry weasel. Now he wanted a breath of fresh air and a word with his friends. Also he was thirsty, and he thought it would be safe to go to the pond for a drink.

He crept out of his hole. He was a dumpy little thing, and his tail really looked far too short for him. He sat for a minute in the sun. It was about noon, and the bank felt warm and comfortable. Then he scampered through the lank, straggling grasses of the bank and went to the edge of the little pond near by. He was careful to keep under the grass as he went, and he did not move even a blade as he ran!

He was drinking from the pond when he heard a movement behind him, and he turned to run at once.

'Stay where you are,' said a squeaky voice. 'I shall not hurt you!'

The field-vole saw a creature about twice as big as he was, with a longer tail. He thought it was a brown rat, one of the many that lived about the pond and hunted fiercely all the year round. He was too frightened to move, and he crouched by the water, staring in fear at the creature just in front of him.

'Do you take me for a rat?' said the water-vole, amused. 'Indeed, I am nothing to do with the rats! I am a vole, like yourself, but as I can swim and dive well my name is *water*-vole. Look at me carefully and you will see I am your big cousin, and not a rat.'

The little field-vole looked at the water-vole and knew at once that he had nothing to fear. His cousin was a big, stumpy fellow, with thick reddish-brown fur in which a few greyish hairs grew. His muzzle was rounded and his tail was much shorter than a rat's.

'Yes, I see you are not a rat,' said the little vole, thankfully. 'Sometimes *I* am mistaken for a mouse.'

'You know,' said the water-vole, pulling a long face, 'it is a dreadful thing to be mistaken for a *rat* – far worse than being thought a mouse. Humans often kill me, thinking I am a water-rat, though I am nothing of the kind. *I* couldn't eat the things a rat eats! I am a harmless little fellow, and I like to eat grass and water-weed. It is very unfortunate indeed that I look like a rat.'

The field-vole felt sorry for his big cousin.

'Do you always live by the water?' he asked.

'Oh yes,' said the water-vole. 'I love the water. I will show you how well I can swim in a minute. My home is in a burrow here, and it has an entrance below the water and an entrance in the bank here, too. At night I come out to feed. I do not usually look for food in the daytime, but this morning was so fine and warm that I could not help coming out to bask in the sunshine. Can I offer you a nice tasty bit of willow shoot?'

33

'Well, I do feel hungry,' said the small field-vole.

'Come along, then, to my dining-table,' said the water-vole. He led the way to the reeds that grew thickly by the side of the pond. In one place he had nibbled off the stems or flattened them, making a kind of platform. This was his dining-table. It was littered with the remains of other meals. The big vole offered the field-vole a tender shoot of willow and a piece of horsetail stem.

'Do you build your nest on this platform?' asked the little vole, looking round.

'I did last year,' said the water-vole, chewing a willow shoot. 'My wife and I made a round nest of reeds and grasses here, and brought up our young ones quite safely. The year before that we built our nest underground, but a flood came and swamped our nursery. Where do *you* build, cousin?'

'Oh, not underground,' said the little vole. 'My wife builds a grassy nest somewhere alongside one of our runs above ground. I store food underground for the cold days. I should like you to come and have a meal with me if you will. I have acorns, beech-mast and a few seeds.'

'I will come,' began the big vole – and then suddenly he stopped and looked frightened. The little vole saw him staring into the air. He looked up and saw, to his amazement, an enormous bird sailing downwards with widespread wings. It was a large grey heron coming down to the pond to fish.

The heron spied the two little voles on the reedy platform, and altered her course. Two tasty morsels for dinner! But the two

34

voles did not wait! The field-vole rushed to the bank and cowered
under a stone, calling in a high, squeaky voice to his big cousin to
come too.

But the water-vole took no notice. He dived straight into the
pond! Plop! it was a beautiful dive. The field-vole watched his
cousin swimming swiftly across the water. He swam with his hind
legs and held his front paws up against his chin. The heron
landed in the water and held her strong beak ready to spear the
little swimmer – but just as the heron pounced downwards the
water-vole dived again! Down into the water he went, and reached
his hole in the bank a good way under water. He scrambled in
and forced his way up the tunnel
to his dry little room above.
There he sat in safety,
gasping in terror.

'It is a good thing I have an entrance underwater!' he thought. 'I should never have escaped if I hadn't had my hole ready for me here. So the heron has come back again! I had better leave this pond for a while. I wonder if my little cousin, the field-vole, would let me share his hole until the heron is gone?'

He waited until the sun had gone and the night had crept over the cold fields. The heron flapped her wings and went away – but the water-vole felt sure that she would come back again soon. It was a favourite pond of hers in the winter-time.

The water-vole crept out of his hole by the above-ground entrance and listened hard. There was not a sound to be heard. The vole was listening for the screech of the barn owl, who loved to hunt at night for mice and voles. But the owl was hunting over another field far away. The water-vole crept through the reeds and ran towards the hedgerow. When he reached the bank, he lifted his blunt muzzle and sniffed gently. He was trying to find the smell of the field-vole. At last he smelt what he wanted, and

followed his nose to the hole where the field-vole lived.

'Are you there, cousin?' he called, softly.

'Oh, is it you?' squeaked a frightened voice, and the little vole came running up to the entrance of his underground tunnel. 'I wondered if that great bird would spear you and kill you. Were you safe?'

'Oh yes,' said the water-vole. 'I swam to the underwater entrance of my home and escaped that way. But I am afraid to live by the pond whilst the heron is there. Will you let me live with you until she has gone? Is there room?'

'Plenty!' cried the little vole, gladly. 'Come in at once, before the stoat hunts the hedgerow. I have food to offer you and a warm room underground.'

The water-vole took a last look round – and then shot into the hole so quickly that the little vole was sent head over heels down the tunnel. He said nothing but, picking himself up, fled with the water-vole down the burrow.

'The stoat!' whispered the water-vole. 'He was there behind me! He pounced – but he only caught the tip of my tail. Dear me, cousin, your bank is just as dangerous as my pond! I think I shall go back tomorrow!'

All that night the two voles crouched together in fright. When the morning came the water-vole looked out and saw that the heron had not come back to the pond. He smelt stoat again and decided to go back to the water.

'Goodbye, cousin,' he said. 'I am more at home in the water, so I think I will go back. But come to me if you are in danger at any time and I will most certainly help you!'

THE END

SLEEPERS
AWAKE!

The month of March was kind to the hedgerow folk. East winds blew, but only gently, and at midday the sun shone down so warmly that the primroses came out by the dozen on the bank under the oak tree. They shone there, pale and yellow, in their rosettes of green leaves. Some early purple violets flowered too, and as little mice ran to and fro they smelt the hidden blossoms in surprise, wondering what the fragrance was.

The creatures of the hedgerow were full of excitement and delight. After the long winter it was glorious to feel the warm fingers of the sun reaching down into hole and burrow. The rabbits leapt about madly. The hedgehog woke up and came out one night, hungry and thirsty, looking for something to eat. The dormouse woke too, quite a different-looking creature from the one that had fallen asleep in the autumn – for now he was thin and flabby.

Under a big stone on the bank was a toad. It was a good hiding-place, moist and sheltered. The toad had used it for his

home for many years, for he was an old fellow, wise and cunning. He had scraped out a small hollow with his back legs, and his body fitted into the hole very well indeed. The big stone jutted out over him, and there he lived, snug and safe.

All the hedgerow folk knew him. The stoat had often sniffed under the big stone as he ran silently by. He could smell toad there. But he did not try to hunt him out. He had been warned against toads by all the older stoats, so he left the big toad alone. The stoat thought that the toad lived a dull life, for all winter long, night and day, the toad never left his stone. There he squatted by himself, unmoving.

But he was not dull. He was asleep. There were no insects about in the winter-time, and he did not like the cold. So he slept deeply, not feeling the cold frost, nor missing his food. No one looking under the stone would see him, for he was as brown as the earth and as still as the stone itself.

But now that March had come, and the air grew warm, the old toad stirred himself. He opened his eyes with difficulty, for his long sleep had stuck the lids together. He rubbed them with one of his front feet, and soon he could see. He sat still for a few minutes, remembering. This was his stone. Outside was the hedgerow. Slugs were to be found in the ditch. Beetles ran on the bank. He was hungry – very hungry. Then he felt something else too – something stronger than hunger. He wanted to get to some water. He wanted to croak loudly and find a nice little toad-wife.

A noise came to his ears. It was the croaking of frogs in the pond nearby! They had woken too, and had come up from the mud at the bottom, excited by the spring sunshine. The toad felt more and more excited. His throat swelled and he gave a hoarse and gurgling croak.

'Oh, so you are awake at last,' said a voice, and a brilliant eye looked under the stone. It belonged to a frog, a large one who had slept the winter through at the bottom of the muddy ditch. He had woken up the day before, and had remembered the toad under the stone. They had often croaked to one another the year before.

'Yes, I'm awake,' said the toad, blinking his beautiful coppery eyes., 'Is the weather very warm?'

'Yes, very,' said the frog, delightedly. 'It is the warmest spring we have had for a long time. There are hundreds of frogs in the pond already. I came to see if you were awake yesterday, but you weren't. Are you coming to the pond?'

'Of course,' said the toad, trying to move his legs, which were stiff after his long sleep. 'Wait for me. My legs are like wood, but they will soon feel right again.'

The frog sat outside in the sunshine, keeping a sharp look-out for any enemy. His bright eyes looked all round him, and his back legs were ready to leap at any moment. His coat was yellowish-green, and matched the grass around him very well. He heard the croaking of the frogs in the pond and he was anxious to join them. It was wonderful to be awake again, warm in the sunshine, with all the excitement of spring-time before him.

The toad stretched out a leg. Then very slowly he crawled forward from under the mossy stone. As he came in to the sunshine, a little shadow passed over him. At once both the frog and the toad sat as if frozen stiff. The shadow was cast by a small fly. It came to rest on a blade of grass just in front of the frog.

From the frog's wide mouth flicked out a long tongue. Its sticky end touched the little fly, and before the insect knew what was happening, the tongue was inside the frog's mouth again, and he was being swallowed. The frog's eyes shut as he swallowed the morsel, and then opened again.

41

'That was good,' he said.
'Very small, but quite good. Our
tongues are useful, don't you think so, toad?'
    The toad agreed. He too had a long tongue fixed cleverly to
the front of his mouth, instead of to the back. It was easy to flick it
out quickly and aim it at any fly or beetle passing near.

'Come,' said the frog, impatiently. 'We must go to the pond.'

The toad crawled right out of his hole under the stone. For a few moments he stayed still, blinking in the glare of the sun. Then he began to move towards the water, crawling along, or making short hops. The frog took enormous leaps, and had to keep waiting for the toad. Soon they came to a puddle. In it were two frogs, croaking excitedly.

'Why don't you go to the big pond instead of wasting your time here?' asked the toad, curiously.

'We might as well lay eggs here,' said the frogs in a croaking chorus. 'Why not?'

'You are foolish,' said the toad. 'Tomorrow this puddle will have dried up – then your eggs will shrivel in the sun and you will have no children.' But the two frogs took no notice. So the toad left them and followed his friend to the pond.

But before they had reached it, there came the sound of scampering feet behind them, and a loud noise sounded above them. It was a dog, barking! He had seen the two creatures moving and had come to chase them. The toad froze down into the grass, and the frog crouched flat beside him, each hoping that the dog would not see them.

The dog, who was not much more than a puppy, sniffed at the frog's moist body. In terror the frog straightened out his long back legs, and sprang high up into the air, hitting the dog's nose as he jumped. He fell to ground and leapt again, this time towards the gleaming pond. Plop! He was safely in it before the dog had recovered from his fright and astonishment.

But the toad could not leap away. He was a slow mover and could not hope to escape an enemy. He lay perfectly still, but over his back tiny drops of moisture began to shine which were oozing out from the knobby warts that covered his brown body. A nasty smell arose from the crouching toad. The dog sniffed it in disgust. This creature did not smell nice. He smelt dangerous. He

43

put his head down to the toad and sniffed again. Then he opened his mouth and cautiously tried to pick up the toad – but as soon as he tasted the toad's back he started back in dismay. What a horrible taste! What a disgusting smell! This creature was poisonous. The dog shook his head to get rid of the taste in his mouth, and then trotted away. Never, never again would he interfere with toads or frogs!

The frog popped his head out of the pond. His big eyes looked scared. Was his friend eaten? No! He was on the bank, quite safe, just about to let himself drop into the water.

The pond was full of croaking, wriggling frogs and toads. The toad looked about for a wife. Soon he met a big brown female toad. Together they sank to the bottom of the pond to choose a place for their eggs. The frog also found a wife for himself, a lively, green-backed creature with a merry, bubbling croak.

The sun shone down all that day and the next. Rabbits came and looked in wonder at the excitement in the pond. The heron flew down, but even she could not quiet the happy creatures. 'Come and look at my eggs!' croaked the toad to the frog, one day, when he met his friend under a water-lily leaf. The frog swam down to the bottom of the pond with him, and gazed in surprise at a double string of jelly which was wound round and round and in and out of the stems of water-plants.

'What a long string of eggs!' he croaked. 'I never lay my eggs in strings. Now come and see mine!'

The toad swam to the surface of the pond with the proud frog. He saw a great bunch of eggs all in a mass of white jelly. Little black specks here and there showed where the tadpoles were growing.

'These eggs were laid at the bottom of the pond,' said the frog. 'But the jelly soon swelled up and floated to the surface so that the sunshine could warm the eggs and hatch them. Look! Over there is some frogspawn that was laid before mine. The tadpoles are hatching out already!'

So they were. The toad saw hundreds of tiny little tailed creatures wriggling about on the jelly mass.

'Soon they will grow big and in a few weeks they will have their legs,' said the frog. 'Hind legs first, and then front legs. Then their tails will disappear, and they will be little frogs, anxious to find a home for themselves in our hedgerow.'

'Toad tadpoles grow their front legs first,' said the old toad. 'It is better to grow front legs first.'

'Not at all,' said the frog. 'All well-brought-up tadpoles grow their hind legs first of all.'

'Croak, croak, croak,' began the toad, angrily, and the frog began to shout too – but suddenly there came a cry of warning: 'Ducks! Ducks!' And down to the pond flew two wild ducks, one a beautiful drake and the other his sober-brown wife. All the frogs and toads at once disappeared, and nothing more was heard about tadpoles and their legs.

'Quack!' said the drake, annoyed. 'Why do frogs always go when we come?' Why, indeed!

THE END

THE
STRANGE EGG

There were many more birds about the hedgerow in April and May than in March, for the nightingales were back again, the willow-wrens had arrived, and the chiff-chaff called his name time after time from the alder trees. The steel-blue swallows had left the warmth of Africa and had returned to the spring-time of Britain. They darted about in the blue sky, crying 'Feetafeetit, feetafeetit' in their pretty, twittering voices.

The big grey cuckoo, with his barred chest, had come back too. He cried 'Cuckoo! Cuckoo!' all day long in the month of May. There were times when the hedgerow folk were tired of his voice, but he still carried on. He tried to shout more loudly than any other cuckoo. The birds thought him strange, for he could not sing, neither could he chirrup or twitter. He spoke with an almost human voice.

Another thing that the birds disliked about the cuckoo was his barred chest, which reminded them of the sparrowhawk who came swooping round the hedgerow to hunt small birds.

Sometimes a sparrow would spy the cuckoo sitting in the oak tree and, seeing the barred chest, would cry 'Chirrup! Chirrup! The hawk is in the oak tree! Come and mob him!'

All the sparrows nearby would fly up, and the chaffinches would go too. What a noise and commotion they made! They would surround the cuckoo and shout at him until he was angry and frightened. Then he would spread his pointed wings and fly away, crying 'Cuckoo!' loudly as he flew.

'*I* knew it was only a cuckoo,' the robin would say, flicking his wings over his back. 'I could have told you that before you began to mob him – but it was good fun to watch you all.'

Just then the brown hedge-sparrow called to the robin: 'Come and see my nest! It is finished!'

'You make a nice nest,' said the robin. 'Mine is good, too. You would never guess where it is!'

'Oh, somewhere peculiar!' said the hedge-sparrow, getting into her nest again, and settling down comfortably.

'It's in an old boot down in the ditch,' said the robin, with a creamy trill. 'I've two eggs there already.'

'Well, go away now,' said the hedge-sparrow, sleepily. 'I'm going to lay an egg. I'm going to sit here and look at the blue sky through the little green leaves that keep moving in the wind, and perhaps my egg will be as blue as the sky I love so much.'

In a week's time the robin visited the little hedge-sparrow
again, and she proudly showed him her eggs. She had four, and
they were indeed as blue as the sky. They were really beautiful.

'One of my eggs has hatched already,' said the robin. 'Tell
me if you see any of those grey squirrels about, hedge-sparrow,
for I am so afraid they will steal my nestlings.'

The hedge-sparrow promised, and kept a look-out for the
squirrels. But for days she did not see one. Neither did her little
brown mate, who sometimes took a turn at sitting on the eggs
when his wife wanted to stretch her wings for a while.

But somebody else came to the hedgerow, looking for birds'
nests – not a squirrel, nor the stoat; not the jay, nor the black
jackdaw. It was the big grey cuckoo, a hen-bird with bright eyes.
The cuckoo peered here and there in the hedge. She looked in
the ditch, but she didn't see the robin's nest. No, she didn't think
of looking inside a dirty old boot!

Then she saw the hedge-sparrow sitting on her nest in the
middle of the green hedgerow. The cuckoo sat up in the
oak tree, quite silent, and watched as best she
could. She heard a twitter of excitement
because one of the blue eggs
had just hatched out.

She heard the two birds chattering in delight to one another, and then the little brown cock-bird sat up on the topmost spray of the hedge and began to sing a pretty little song to tell everyone that at last an egg had hatched out into a tiny chick.

The cuckoo made a bubbling noise in her throat, and flew down to the ground. She sat there for a while and then stood up and looked down at the egg she had just laid. It was a surprisingly small egg for such a big bird as the cuckoo. It was a bluish colour, but not so blue as the hedge-sparrow's wonderful eggs.

The cuckoo saw the cock and hen hedge-sparrow fly out of the hedge to find food for the newly-hatched youngster. This was her chance. Taking her egg in her big beak she flew to the hedgerow. She forced her way in to the hidden nest and carefully put her own egg there. Looking round, she saw the hen hedge-sparrow flying back, and she hurriedly picked up one of the bright-blue eggs and flew off with it, leaving her own egg amongst the others in the nest.

She dropped the hedge-sparrow's egg on the ground. It smashed, but the cuckoo paid no heed. She had done what she wanted to do – put her egg into another bird's nest. Now she wouldn't have the trouble of sitting on it, or of looking after the young one when it hatched out!

The wise old toad watched the cuckoo flying hurriedly away, and saw the yellow splash of the dropped egg in the grass. He crawled over to it and flicked out his long tongue to taste the egg. The hedgehog appeared and ran over to it too, for she dearly loved the taste of an egg.

'That's the cuckoo up to her old tricks again,' said the toad, who knew nearly everything about the hedgerow creatures, for he had lived so long.

'She's a wicked creature to give other birds the trouble of rearing her young ones,' said the hedgehog.

'Ah well, it's their own fault,' said the wise toad. 'It is said that she started her bad ways long long ago, because the other birds wouldn't let her nest. They thought she was like a hawk, you know, and pulled her nest to pieces every time she started to build – so in the end she gave up and put her egg into someone else's nest instead.'

The hen hedge-sparrow had flown back to her nest by this time, and had once more settled down on it. She had given the eggs a glance, and had not even noticed that one seemed a little different – not so blue and just a little bigger than the rest. She felt sure they were all her eggs.

She was very happy. Her eggs were hatching, her little mate sang to her often and brought her titbits, and the weather was sunny and warm. One by one the youngsters came out of their eggs, and last of all the cuckoo's egg hatched.

The tiny cuckoo was a strange-looking creature. He was black, bare and ugly, and dear me, he was the hungriest of all! He had a loud voice, and the hen hedge-sparrow was so alarmed at his cries of hunger that she went off to find grubs as well as her mate, leaving the nest with the four babies at the bottom.

The young cuckoo felt uncomfortable. A tiny hedge-sparrow was pressing against his back and he could not bear to feel it. He fell into such a fit of rage that his whole body stiffened itself and his tiny wings stretched out. Somehow he got the other little bird into a hollow on his back and, as soon as he felt him there, he began to climb slowly up the edge of the nest, backwards, using his wings as hands. It was strange to see him. The blackbird, who was sitting on a branch above, was amazed, but it was not her nest, so she said nothing.

At last the cuckoo reached the top of the nest. He gave a shake and the young hedge-sparrow rolled over the edge and fell through the hedge to the ground below, cheeping piteously. The cuckoo sank back to the bottom of the nest, and lay there, quite exhausted. The hen hedge-sparrow, fearing the grey squirrels, flew back to her nest. There was no squirrel there, so she sat down and covered the three young ones with her wings. She did not seem to miss the poor little fledgling nor hear its cheeping from outside the nest.

The cock-bird came back to the hedgerow and saw the little bird on the ground, quite helpless – but he took no notice of it. He did not think it could be one of his little ones. Only the robin was sad and upset. It was impossible, he knew, to carry a young one back to its nest once it had fallen, but a robin is tender-hearted, and he was sad to hear its little cheepings. He hopped over to it and looked at it with his head on one side – but soon he flew away quickly, crying 'Stoat! Stoat!'

The stoat too had heard the shrill cheep-cheep of the little nestling. It snapped up the tiny bird, and ran on its way again, resolving to come that way on the following morning.

Sure enough, the next day there was another little hedge-sparrow baby tipped out of the nest by the cuckoo – and on the following day the third one lay on the ground, cheeping sadly. The stoat ate them all.

And now there was only the little cuckoo left in the nest. It was content. It lay there, fat and happy, for it had all the food brought to the nest. The two hedge-sparrows were proud of their enormous child. They did not seem to notice that the others had all gone. They sang all day about the large nestling and many birds came too look at it.

'He is so big, so strong!' sang the little birds, proudly. 'He is the biggest hedge-sparrow that ever lived! He eats like a big jay,

52

and calls as loudly as a rook!'

The little cuckoo certainly had a harsh and piercing voice. He was always hungry and called all day long. The robins in the ditch became so tired of his voice that to silence him they too fed him, bringing him grubs and the large and hairy woolly-bear caterpillars that he loved so much.

At last the cuckoo had to leave the nest, for he had grown far too big for it! He was three times the size of the hedge-sparrows now, and when they brought him food, they stood on his shoulder to give it to him! It was a strange sight to see. But the hedge-sparrows were delighted with the baby cuckoo. They thought him truly marvellous, and talked about him to everyone in the hedgerow.

One day the old toad saw the cuckoo on the grass pecking at a worm. He blinked his coppery eyes and croaked deeply when the cock hedge-sparrow sang to tell him that the big bird was his nestling.

'Urrrrk, urrrrk!' said the toad, widely. 'If that's a hedge-sparrow, friend, then you are a cuckoo!' And not another word would he say to the puzzled little hedge-sparrow!

THE END

53

THE
WICKED RAT

The hedgerow was quiet in the hot afternoon sun of July. The far-away hills were very blue, and the few clouds in in the sky were silver-white. The pond was as blue as the sky and not even the little black moorhen chick was to be seen making ripples on the surface. It was too hot to sing – too hot to chirrup – too hot to stir from the shelter of the hedgerow! The big oak tree stood quite still, and not even a leaf moved, for there was no breeze anywhere.

The cuckoo no longer called from the woods. Even the small yellowhammer who loved to sing about his 'little bit of bread and *no* cheese', sitting on the telegraph wires by the oak tree, was too hot to open his beak. Everything was drowsy, half-asleep in the hot sun, peaceful and contented.

But no – someone was astir after all! Someone came running down the ditch; a long grey-brown form with a sharp muzzle, big ears and long tail. It was the wicked rat, friend to no one, hungry and fierce.

The hedgerow folk had almost forgotten the rat during the winter. He had lived about the farm then, picking up a good living in the corn-stacks. He had found the farmer's buried mangolds and had gnawed hundreds of them. But when the warm days came he had left them and gone out into the fields. For one thing, the farmer's three kittens had now grown into big, sharp-clawed cats, and the rat was afraid of them. For another thing, the farmer was sensible and had killed no weasels, for he knew that weasels like a meal of rats. So three weasels had come hunting about the farmyard and the rat had run away. He was very much afraid of the fierce little creatures.

He had gone to the hedgerow. There he had made his runs, and had burrowed under the hedge in one place. He had made runs in the soft earth by the pond, too, and there were many holes there that mice and lizards would not go near because they knew that the wicked rat might pounce on them at any moment.

The rat was cruel. He was fierce, brave, clever. Not one of the hedgerow folk could get the better of him, not even the stoat who sometimes came along the ditch to see what he could find. Once a weasel came too, but the rat smelt him a good way off and, long before the weasel came into sight, the rat had disappeared and could not be found.

The hedgerow folk grumbled bitterly to the little field mice, for they were the small cousins of the rat.

'Why do you not tell him to go away? He is a hateful creature. He has no kindness in him, not even to his own family.'

'That is true,' said the long-tailed field mouse. 'I know that he eats his own children sometimes, and if he finds a rat that is ill or hurt, he will eat him too. He is wicked. Even the humans hate him, for they say he brings illness to them. But what can *I* do? He might eat me if I ask him to go away!'

The hedgerow folk went on grumbling, but nobody dared to do anything. The rat lived unmolested in the hedgerow, and had already brought up two families there, watched over by his fierce wife. Now there were nineteen rats about the hedgerow and nothing and nobody was safe.

The robin's second eggs had been eaten by the rats. Three young birds belonging to the freckled thrush had been eaten, and two of the little moorhen chicks had gone the same way. The moorhen was very angry about it and cried out loudly when she saw what the rat was doing. But she could not stop him. After that she made her chicks keep close to her by night and day.

The rabbits complained that many of their young ones had been killed, and one mother rabbit was wild with grief when she found that the rat had discovered her hidden burrow and had eaten all her pretty youngsters so cosily nestled there.

The rat cared for nobody. He was not a friendly animal. He thought of only one thing, and that was where to get his next meal.

On this hot July afternoon the little field mouse was sitting, half-asleep, at the entrance to his burrow. It was in the warm bank. Far below, hidden at the end of the burrow, was his tiny mate, curled up in a nest of dry grass with her new family of youngsters, five pretty little mice like herself. She was very happy. The year before she had built her nest under a big tuft of grass in the hedge, but she had been afraid to bring up her young ones above ground whilst the rats were about. So this summer she had made an underground nursery for them.

'This burrow would be a good place to rest in for the winter,' she thought to herself, sleepily. 'We could store hips and haws here, and some acorns too. I remember last autumn that there were plenty of red hips in the hedgerow above. I climbed up into the branches and picked some, and nibbled out the seeds inside. I took an old nest belonging to the hedge-sparrow for my dining-table.'

Suddenly the little mouse pricked up her small ears. She could hear her mate squeaking at the entrance to the burrow.

He was being very brave indeed – for he was talking to the wicked rat. The rat had come running silently along the ditch, making his way unseen beneath the tall grasses and green nettles.

He had leapt up on to the bank and had suddenly seen the little field mouse.

The mouse stiffened, and then bravely called out to the rat:

'Cousin rat! You have done much harm to the folk of the hedgerow. You have killed and eaten us! Your large family is bringing fear and terror to all the little creatures that live here. Go back to the farm and return no more.'

The fierce rat stopped in surprise. He was hungry. His nose moved as he sniffed the smell of mouse.

'Have you a family?' he asked.

'Never mind whether I have a family or not,' said the small mouse, in alarm, thinking of his tiny wife and tinier youngsters. 'Hear what I say, cousin, or we hedgerow folk will tell the weasel of you and you will be hunted even as you hunt us!'

The rat did not listen. He could smell the little mice down in the burrow, and his whiskers quivered with delight. He suddenly made a spring at the small mouse, who, squeaking with terror, tore down his hole.

Then the hot, peaceful afternoon was filled with the pitiful squealings and squeakings of the mouse family. The rat forced his way into the burrow and went straight to where the mouse was curled up about her family. He snatched at them with his sharp teeth, and before many seconds had passed each of the baby mice was gone. The mother squealed in anger and flung herself on the rat, biting him on the neck. But he easily shook her off, nipped her behind the ears and then ate her too.

When the other mouse saw this he fled down another tunnel, wailing as if his small heart would break. All who heard him made way for him and then ran themselves, for they knew that some great disaster had happened.

The rat was happy. He sniffed around the hole for a few

seconds and then went out again. He found a tuft of grass and lay under it for a little while, enjoying the hot sun. He was satisfied.

The little field mouse was bitterly unhappy. He was full of hatred for the false and treacherous rat; he missed his pretty little wife and longed for his small youngsters. He touched no food that day, and when night came he went to cool himself under a big stone on the bank. There he found the toad, also cooling himself.

'The wicked rat has taken my little mate and my small mice,' said the mouse, twitching his nose as he remembered.

'It is time that the rat went away,' said the toad, slowly. 'He is the enemy of the whole world.'

'You are wise,' said the long-tailed mouse, looking at the toad with sad little eyes. 'Tell me how to get rid of the wicked rat. Who will do that for us? The stoat cannot catch him and if the weasel comes, he knows, and disappears.'

'I remember once before,' said the old toad, blinking his round eyes, 'I remember once before that rats came to this hedgerow and brought death and grief with them. And I remember who destroyed them.'

'Who?' asked the little mouse, eagerly. 'Tell me!'

'It was the brown owl,' said the toad, remembering. 'Yes, he came night after night and watched silently for the rats. And one by one they went.'

'Let us send to the brown owl,' said the mouse. 'He lives in the woods, for I have sometimes heard him hooting. We will send the blackbird tomorrow.'

The blackbird was glad to go and fetch the brown owl, for the rat had tried to kill one of her nestlings in June. She flew to the woods and hunted for him, long and hard. The noisy jays told her that the owl was hiding in a pine tree, close up to the trunk, his eyes half-closed. There the blackbird found him and told him of the rats.

'I will come,' said the wise owl, opening his great eyes. 'Tonight I will come. I have a wife and five hungry youngsters, and I shall be glad of food to take to them.'

That night the hedgerow folk heard the brown owl hooting. 'Ooooooooooo!' he called 'Oo-oo-oo-*ooo*!' It was a beautiful sound through the dark night, but all the little mice shivered, for they were as much afraid of the owl as were the rats. They kept close inside their holes – but the rats were out hunting.

The brown owl flew on widespread wings to the hedgerow. He flew silently, so silently that no one heard him except the little field-mouse who was listening anxiously in his hole down in the bank.

The owl flew right over the hedgerow. He looked down with his great eyes. There was no moon and the stars gave only the very faintest of light – but it was quite enough for the owl to see by. He was watching for the tiniest movements of the grasses which would show him where a rat ran.

Soon he saw what he was looking for! The grass moved a little – and at the same moment the owl dropped like a stone, feet foremost. His talons closed over a struggling body – it was the rat!

It was useless for the wicked rat to try to escape. He was

caught in a trap – for the owl's feet closed like a vice. The brown owl flew off with the rat and gave him to his hungry mate. Then back he came again to the hedgerow – and before the night was gone seven rats had been caught and taken to the nest in the old hollow tree.

The rest of the rats fled in terror, far from the hedgerow. 'Brown owl!' they squealed to one another. 'Brown owl!'

And once again the small hedgerow folk lived in peace. The long-tailed mouse found another wife and had a second family – and when they wanted to run out of the burrow too soon he would say 'Come back! The wicked rat will get you! Aha! The wicked rat!'

THE END

THE
Enid Blyton
TRUST FOR CHILDREN

We hope you have enjoyed the nature stories in this book. Next time you are out walking in the countryside, please think for a moment about those children who are too ill to do the exciting things that you and your friends do.

Help them by sending a donation, large or small, to the ENID BLYTON TRUST FOR CHILDREN. The Trust will use all your gifts to help children who are sick or handicapped and need to be made happy and comfortable.

Please send your postal orders or cheques to:

The Enid Blyton Trust For Children,
International House,
1 St Katherine's Way,
London E1 9UN.

Thank you very much for your help.